THE WRESTLING SEASON

A Play
by
LAURIE BROOKS

Dramatic Publishing
Woodstock, Illinois • England • Australia • New Zealand

*** NOTICE ***

For Joanna
Brave and Beautiful
and
For Jeff Church
Who made the play and the playwright stronger

* * * *

Acknowledgments

For support and nourishment, my love and appreciation to Jeff Church, Leigh Miller, the fabulous UMKC cast, Brooke, Joette and the entire Coterie Theatre family, The Children's Theatre Foundation of America, John Shorter, Manhasset High School Theatre Department, Peter Guastella, Manhasset High School wrestling coach, Phillip John Kinen and the Shawnee Mission High School Theatre Department, The Kennedy Center's New Visions/New Voices 1998, Mary Hall Surface, Lowell Swortzell and the New York University Program in Educational Theatre's Summer Reading Series at The Provincetown Playhouse 1999, clinical psychologist Sidney Horowitz, novelist John Irving, and especially my daughters, Joanna, Liz and Stephanie.

The Wrestling Season was developed at The Kennedy Center's 1998 New Visions/New Voices: A Forum for New Works in Progress for Young Audiences, and the New York University Program in Educational Theatre's Summer Reading Series at The Provincetown Playhouse, 1999.

The Wrestling Season was featured at New Visions 2000/One Theatre World, a National Festival of Theatre for Young people and Families at The Kennedy Center, Washington, D.C.

Laurie Brooks was the recipient of a 1999 Aurand Harris grant to The Coterie for *The Wrestling Season*, awarded by The Children's Theatre Foundation of America.

The Wrestling Season was developed and featured at the 1998 New Visions/New Voices: A Forum for New Plays-in-Progress for Young Audiences, at The John F. Kennedy Center in Washington, D.C., May 1998. The production was directed by Jeff Church. It was commissioned by The Coterie Theatre, Kansas City, Missouri.

CAST

Jolt	TOM COSTELLO
Willy	REGGIE HARRIS
Luke	ANDREAS KRAEMER
Matt	LAFONTAINE ELITE OLIVER
Melanie	BONNIE WAGGONER
Heather	JODY FLADER
Nicole	RISA GREEN
Kori	MEGAN GILBRIDE
Referee	MATT SAWYER

PRODUCTION STAFF

DEREK E. GORDON .... Vice President for Education, Executive Producer

KIM PETER KOVAC .... Program Manager, Youth and Family Programs, NV/NV Producer

DIEDRE KELLY LAVRAKAS .. Production Operations Manager NV/NV Casting Director/Production Manager

JOHN "SCOOTER" KRATTENMAKER .... Stage Manager

In 1999, *The Wrestling Season* was further developed at New York University, School of Education, Department of Music and Performing Arts Professions Program in Educational Theatre and presented at Staged Readings of New Plays for Young Audiences, The Provincetown Playhouse, New York, N.Y. The production was directed by Jeff Church and included the following artists:

CAST

Matt .... SHANNON GANNON
Luke .... JOHN JEFFREY MARTIN
Willy .... GERARD T. SCOTT
Jolt .... DENNIS WALTERS
Heather .... LAUREN O'BRIEN
Nicole .... MARIA ELENA LOPEZ-FRANK
Melanie .... SIDNEY AUSTIN
Kori .... AMANDA RAFUSE
Referee .... JIM GROLLMAN
Stage Directions .... DANA LEVIN

PRODUCTION STAFF

Producer .... JEFF KENNEDY
Stage Manager .... JOHN DEL GAUDIO
Lighting Design .... JASON LIVINGSTON
Production Supervisor .... LOWELL SWORTZELL

The Wrestling Season's world premiere was at The Coterie Theatre, Kansas City, Missouri, January 2000. The production was directed by Jeff Church and included the following artists:

CAST

Referee .... ANTHONY GUEST
Luke............................. JOSHUA F. DECKER
Kori........................... MELANNA D. GRAY
Melanie .... BETH GUEST
Nicole .... ALICIA JENKINS-EWING
Matt......................... DAVID MCNAMARA
Jolt............................. JUDSON MORGAN
Heather .... AMANDA RAFUSE
Willy .... MATT RAMSEY

PRODUCTION STAFF

Associate Director/Wrestling Coach ...... LEIGH MILLER
Set and Costume Design/Properties .... ELIZA CAIN
Lighting Design .... ART KENT
Sound Design .... DAVID KIEHL
Production Stage Manager .... BROOKE SCHEPPNER
Scenic Construction .... DAN ESLINGER

Playwright's Notes:

The action of the play is seamless, moving from one scene to another unencumbered by sets and costume changes. Much will be left to the audience's imagination. The ensemble functions as a chorus when they are not in the playing space, responding to the action onstage as a group, in pairs and individually. All eight young people wear wrestling singlets and wrestling shoes throughout the play.

Movement in the scenes suggests wrestling moves, holds and escapes. When the stage directions read, "Ensemble shifts," they form new physical arrangements to underscore the action.

Wrestling weight classes in the play can be adjusted according to the actors' approximate size and current high school wrestling rules.

The referee is an integral part of the play throughout, moving about the mat as if each scene is a wrestling match.

Entrances and exits on and off the mat should be used to further define relationships between the characters.

The action between Matt and Melanie on page 45 is an act of sexual agression, but it is not rape.

OFFICIAL WRESTLING SIGNALS
HIGH SCHOOL AND COLLEGE

Reprinted with permission of the National Federation of State High School Associations.

THE WRESTLING SEASON

A Play in One Act
For 5 Men and 4 Women

CHARACTERS

MATT................................. 17 years old
KORI................................. 17 years old
MELANIE..................... 17, "Cherry" Garcia
LUKE .... 17, Matt's best friend
HEATHER .... 17, Jolt's girlfriend
JOLT................................. 17, wrestler
WILLY .... 17, about the same size as Matt
NICOLE .... 17, Heather's friend
REFEREE .... wears black and white referee uniform,
and carries a whistle

SETTING: A bare stage. Standard-issue wrestling mat at center.

THE WRESTLING SEASON

(Lights. All nine characters are grouped on the mat.

ENSEMBLE FUNCTIONS AS A CHORUS.)

ALL *(except REFEREE).* I will remember always that fair play, moral obligation and ethics are a part of winning and losing, that graciousness and humility should always characterize a winner and that pride and honor do not desert a good loser.

(The ensemble explodes out into the space. They remain present throughout the play, watching and commenting on the action.)

HEATHER. You think you know the way it is.
JOLT. You think you know the score.
NICOLE. You think you're so smart.
KORI. You think you've got me figured out.
WILLY. You think you've got me pegged. Pinned.
MELANIE. You think you know me, but you don't.
LUKE. How can you know me?
MATT. I'm not even sure I know myself.

(REF blows whistle. MATT, LUKE, JOLT and WILLY warm up. REF blows whistle, indicates MATT and

*LUKE. They take positions and the practice match be-
gins. The ensemble yells, "Take him down!" "Push him!
Push him!" and "Go! Go! Go!" Each wrestler struggles
to take the other down. MATT flips LUKE onto his back.
REF signals two points. LUKE tries to escape. MATT
pins him. REF counts "One, two..." slaps the mat to
signal a pin. Buzzer.)*

MATT. And now I'd like to thank all the little people who
have helped me to attain my goals.

LUKE. Save it for the media.

MATT. I'd like to thank my mom for believing in me, my
coach for kicking my butt...

LUKE. I think I'm gonna be sick.

MATT. ...and last but not least, my buddy Luke, inspira-
tion and guiding force.

LUKE. Next time you'll beg for mercy.

MATT. In your dreams.

LUKE. I wrestle slicker than you any day.

MATT. You won't have to worry about outsmarting me
this year.

LUKE. I never worry about outsmarting you.

MATT. I mean, I won't be a threat at 171. I talked to
Coach this morning. I'm gonna weigh in at 160 this season.

LUKE. You're kiddin'.

MATT. Dead serious.

LUKE. You're gonna be unstoppable at 160.

MATT. Yeah. It was Mom's idea.

LUKE. She wants that scholarship more than you do.

MATT. Nobody wants it more than I do. Here's the plan.
Drop weight to 160, train like a madman for that slot,

kick ass in the wrestle-offs, win the divisionals, then the regional championship, then the state finals. One. Two. Three.

LUKE. Easy as that?

MATT. I didn't say it'd be easy.

LUKE. Good, because you gotta pass pre-calc to stay on the team.

MATT. Thanks, Mom.

LUKE. You're gonna need major help to pull up that pre-calc grade.

MATT. You got me through Algebra III, didn't you?

LUKE. Yeah, that was a minor miracle.

MATT. If I can keep my concentration, I'll be home free. Like Coach says...

LUKE. ...don't need to be the best, you just gotta win.

MATT. One match at a time.

LUKE. And pass pre-calc.

MATT. Yeah. I'm counting on you for that.

LUKE. And lose the weight and keep it off.

(MATT wrestles LUKE.)

MATT. Wait a minute. Is this encouragement?

LUKE. This is realism.

MATT. I'll do whatever it takes, okay? I'll do extra workouts. I'll visualize my goals. I'll fast and meditate like those demented monks over in Tibet. I want this.

LUKE. Quarter finals weren't good enough for you, huh?

MATT. I've gotta go all the way this year if I want a scholarship. This is my future we're talking about here.

LUKE. You forgot one minor detail. If you drop down to
  the 160 slot, you gotta get past Willy in the wrestle-offs.
  He's good.

MATT. Yeah, but he's not slick. I'll out-maneuver him. I
  learned to kick your butt, didn't I?

LUKE. Yeah. Only because I taught you all my moves in
  old man Gebhardt's garage.

MATT. The sacred training ground. Seems like a hundred
  years ago.

LUKE. Yeah. Remember how we drilled those reversals?

MATT. I remember how scrawny you were.

LUKE. Oh, yeah?

MATT. Yeah.

LUKE. Scrawny? I don't think so.

  *(LUKE wrestles MATT. Buzzer. Ensemble shifts. REF
  blows whistle, indicates MATT and LUKE.)*

MATT. Come on. We're gonna be late.

LUKE. Late for what?

MATT. I told you about ten times. My mom's expecting
  you for dinner.

LUKE. Power bars and yogurt? I'm not hungry.

MATT. Will you lighten up? What's going on with you
  lately?

LUKE. Nothing.

MATT. I'm pretty sure it's not nothing.

LUKE. I've got a paper due on Monday and that lab re-
  port's killing me.

MATT. You work too hard, my friend. You need to have
  some fun. *(LUKE sobs silently.)* Hey. Come on, man.
  Come on. It can't be that bad.

LUKE. How would you know how bad it is.

MATT. 'Cause I'm the best friend you got in the world?

LUKE. You don't have a clue, okay?

MATT. So enlighten me.

LUKE. You wouldn't understand.

MATT. If you're trying to insult me, you've succeeded.

LUKE. I'm not trying to insult you.

MATT. What, then? Did I do something?

LUKE. It's not you. It's me. Just forget it. Let's go.

MATT. No. I'm not going to forget it. Whatever this is, it's really got to you. Tell me.

LUKE. You know how you got this plan? You can see your whole year in front of you.

MATT. Yeah...

LUKE. You got your whole future figured out.

MATT. Yeah...

LUKE. Well, I don't have anything figured out. I don't have a plan.

MATT. You don't need a plan. You're ten times smarter than I am. You can have your pick of schools next year and scholarships, too. You're ugly, but looks aren't everything. You've got it all, man.

LUKE. You don't know.

MATT. I know everything there is to know about you and some things you don't even know about yourself.

(REF blows whistle, indicates LUKE in spotlight.)

LUKE. You think you know me, but you don't.

(REF blows whistle twice to resume scene. Ensemble shifts.)

MATT. I know. It's some girl, right?

LUKE. No.

MATT. Is it the team? Are you worried about the wrestle-offs?

LUKE. No. Jolt'll probably kick my butt.

MATT. Maybe not. We'll train together. In Gebhardt's garage, like the old days.

LUKE. It doesn't matter. Nothing really matters now.

MATT. Hey. Don't say that. It'll be all right. *(Reaches out to LUKE. LUKE grabs MATT, hugs him.)* It's okay. Whatever it is, it'll be all right.

(Buzzer. REF blows whistle, indicates JOLT and WILLY.)

JOLT. They're mighty friendly.

WILLY. Too friendly, if you ask me.

JOLT. I didn't ask you.

WILLY. Too bad. Guess you don't want to hear the news about Mr. Can't Do Wrong and his sidekick.

JOLT. What news?

WILLY. I don't think I heard you ask me.

JOLT. I heard he's after your wrestling slot, if that's what you mean. Coach said he's dropping weight to the 160 slot. Trouble for you.

WILLY. I can take him.

JOLT. Yeah, you and who else? He's tough. And look how he's muscled up since last year.

WILLY. Do I look worried?

JOLT. You should be.

WILLY. He's nothin' but an ass-kisser.

JOLT. Yeah, he's on Coach's A-list, all right.

WILLY. If Coach only knew.

JOLT. Knew what?

WILLY. Was that a question?

JOLT. All right. What about Mr. Can't Do Wrong and his
sidekick?

WILLY. I know the truth about those perverts.

JOLT. What truth?

WILLY. They're too sweet for their own good, if you
know what I mean. They got it bad for each other.

JOLT. Yeah?

WILLY. It's so obvious.

JOLT. Yeah. How can you tell?

WILLY. Can't you?

JOLT. Sure I can. I can always tell. But do you have any
proof?

WILLY. Yeah. I do.

JOLT. You've got proof?

WILLY. Yeah.

JOLT. Right. You're so full of it.

WILLY. I saw them. In the locker room. They were all
over each other.

JOLT. What were they doing?

WILLY. What do you think? *(REF blows whistle, signals
#20, says, "Unsportsmanlike Conduct.")* It was disgust-
ing.

*(REF indicates HEATHER and NICOLE, who join
WILLY and JOLT on the mat.)*

HEATHER. What was disgusting?

WILLY. You don't wanna know.

NICOLE. I do.

HEATHER. I do, too.

JOLT. I'll tell you later tonight when we're alone.

HEATHER. My parents'll be home tonight.

JOLT. Then I'll meet you at the library.

HEATHER. Eight o'clock. Reference.

JOLT. I got somethin' you can refer to.

NICOLE. Would somebody please tell me what was disgusting?

WILLY. Come here. I'll show you.

NICOLE. Uh-uh. I don't wanna know that bad.

WILLY. Come on. Just a little closer.

NICOLE. Tell me from a distance, okay?

WILLY. That takes all the fun out of it.

NICOLE. For you, maybe.

(JOLT and HEATHER whisper together.)

WILLY. You're hurting my feelings.

NICOLE. You'll get over it.

HEATHER *(to JOLT)*. You're kidding!

JOLT. Do I look like I'm kidding?

HEATHER. I never would have thought that. Never!

JOLT. It's true. Willy's got proof.

HEATHER. Oh, my God.

JOLT. Willy saw them together.

NICOLE. Saw who?

HEATHER. You mean together together?

WILLY. Yeah. Well...sort of.

HEATHER. Well, either you saw them or you didn't.

JOLT. I told you. He saw them. In the locker room.

HEATHER. Oh, my God!

NICOLE. Saw who?

HEATHER. Well, it makes perfect sense if you think of it. They're always together.

NICOLE. If you don't tell me this instant who you're talking about, I'm going to scream.

HEATHER. Matt and Luke, of course.

NICOLE. Matt and Luke?

HEATHER. That's why Matt doesn't have a girl.

WILLY. Who'd have him?

NICOLE. I would. But he's not interested in me.

HEATHER. That's what I mean. That's the point.

NICOLE. He's always hanging out with Luke.

HEATHER. And Kori. Why else would he hang out with those two?

NICOLE. What do you mean?

HEATHER. Well, Kori's not exactly Miss America. All that chopped-off hair and those weird hanging things she calls jewelry.

NICOLE. Yeah, she's scary.

HEATHER. She must shop at the junkyard.

NICOLE. And you know her and food.

HEATHER. Have you ever seen her at a dessert table?

(REF blows whistle, indicates KORI in spotlight.)

KORI. You think you know me, but you don't.

(REF blows whistle twice to resume action. Ensemble shifts.)

NICOLE. So what about Matt and Luke?

HEATHER. God, Nicki, do we have to draw you a picture?

WILLY. Those guys give me the creeps.

NICOLE. What guys?

JOLT. Especially Mr. Can't Do Wrong. I'm glad you're wrestling him.

WILLY. Yeah, but you gotta wrestle Luke.

NICOLE. Matt and Luke what?

HEATHER. Come on, Nicki, I'll tell you all about it.

(Buzzer. Ensemble shifts, whispering to one another. MATT jumps rope double time. REF blows whistle, indicates MATT and LUKE. LUKE sees MATT, turns to leave.)

MATT. Hey, wait.

LUKE. What?

MATT. I'm down to 162. Two pounds to go.

LUKE. Your mom's not coping too well. She called me.

MATT. What did she say?

LUKE. She's worried you're killing yourself. She wanted me to tell her what to do to get you to eat.

MATT. What'd you say?

LUKE. I told her to get off your back about scholarships.

MATT. Right. You said that.

LUKE. I didn't but I should have. I gotta go.

MATT. I thought you were gonna work out. Isn't that why you came in here?

LUKE. I forgot something.

MATT. What? *(LUKE picks up a towel at the edge of the mat.)* That's what you forgot? A towel?

LUKE. No.

MATT. What then?

LUKE. What is this—twenty questions? I don't have to answer to you.

MATT. You can stop the act now because I know.

LUKE. Know what?

MATT. What do you think?

LUKE. I've gotta go.

MATT. You can't stand to be in the same room with me, can you?

LUKE. What are you talking about?

MATT. It's not my fault.

LUKE. I know that.

MATT. Then why are you avoiding me?

LUKE. I'm not avoiding you.

MATT. Oh, no? I came to pick you up this morning and you'd already left. You managed to get to pre-calc late and leave early.

LUKE. They wrote faggot on my locker.

(Silence.)

MATT. Do you know who did it?

LUKE. I've got a pretty good idea.

MATT. Doesn't take a rocket scientist to figure it out.

LUKE. It won't come off.

MATT. Willy better watch himself in the wrestle-offs, 'cause I'm gonna hurt him for this.

LUKE. I gotta go.

MATT. You gonna help me study tonight for that pre-calc test?

LUKE. I can't.

MATT. I thought you said you'd help me.

LUKE. I'm not responsible for your grades. I've got my own studying to do.

MATT. Liar. This thing's got to you worse than me. We gotta stick together, man, or they'll win. That's what this is all about. Wrestling. One slot per weight class. They want our slots, man.

LUKE. No, that's what this is about for you.

MATT. You bet. It's wrestling season.

LUKE. The whole world is about you and wrestling.

MATT. Right now, yeah.

LUKE. I'm outta here.

MATT *(grabs LUKE)*. Luke, wait.

LUKE. Get off me.

(MATT makes an elaborate gesture of letting go of LUKE's arm.)

MATT. You think it's true, don't you? You believe it. *(LUKE laughs.)* It's not funny. You think I want you like that? Is that what you think of me?

LUKE. You? It's all about you, isn't it? Whatever it takes to get what you want.

(REF blows whistle, signals #10, says, "Potentially Dangerous." LUKE throws the towel, exits off mat. MATT jumps rope. Ensemble stares at MATT, whispers. Someone points. There is laughter. JOLT gives out with a long, slow, wolf whistle.)

MATT. Okay. I'm gay. Is that what you want to hear?

(Ensemble shifts. MATT jumps rope. REF indicates KORI and MATT.)

KORI. You don't have to shout. We can all hear you.

MATT. Don't start, Kori. I don't want to talk about it.

KORI. Okay.

MATT. I gotta stay focused. I can't let them get to me. Not even Luke.

KORI. Okay.

MATT. They stare at me like I'm some kind of freak.

KORI. Who?

MATT. Everyone. They stare at me and then look away real fast when I see them. Like they're waiting for me to do something.

KORI. I thought you didn't want to talk about it.

MATT. It's like I've done something wrong, but I don't know what it is.

KORI. It's not about what you have or haven't done.

MATT. Even Coach treated me different today, like ... I don't know, like I was someone else. I wanted to kill somebody.

KORI. You guys don't get it, do you? You're entertainment, that's all. So what if you are gay?

MATT. I'm not gay. And neither is Luke.

KORI. What if you were? What's the big deal? You're the same person either way, aren't you?

(HEATHER and NICOLE shift.)

HEATHER. Well, it figures. They're always together. And Luke's kind of ... *(Flops her wrist)* Well, you know.

NICOLE. Heather!

HEATHER. Well, it's the truth.

NICOLE. That's not very nice.

HEATHER. Nice? How boring can you get?

KORI *(to HEATHER)*. It's too bad you have no life. I guess you have to make up stories about everyone else's just to have something to talk about.

HEATHER. Kori, you wouldn't recognize a life if it jumped up and bit you.

NICOLE. Ooooo.

HEATHER. Don't pay any attention to her, Nicki, she's a non-person.

(HEATHER and NICOLE shift.)

KORI. Heather and her minions. It's a power thing. Makes her the main attraction and she knows it.

MATT. But everyone believes her.

KORI. It's too much fun not to believe her.

MATT. I gotta do something. I can't stand it. I can't concentrate.

KORI. Well, you could kill Heather. I'll assist you on that one.

MATT. Yeah, let's smother her with her hair.

KORI. I was kidding, Matt. Just let it go. That's what I do when they talk about me. *(She imitates.)* "Hey, Kori's parents are drug addicts. They did so much acid in the Sixties their brains are fried. I heard she wears thong underwear. I heard she never changes her underwear. I heard she doesn't wear any underwear." Remember when they said I stripped at a party and danced buck-naked for everybody there.

MATT. I knew that wasn't true. I was there.

KORI. What about that time in ninth grade that money was missing and everyone accused me of taking it.

MATT. That was bad, but it's not the same. It's not personal.

KORI. I took being labeled a thief personal.

MATT. I hear them talking in my head. Whole conversations. That's what gets me. I know what they're thinking.

KORI. Because you've thought the same thing about somebody else, right?

MATT. Wrong.

KORI. Come on. You hate the whole idea of being gay.

MATT. I'm glad I'm not.

KORI. Because that makes you better?

MATT. I didn't say that.

KORI. You feel sorry for them? Is that it?

MATT. Whose side are you on, anyway?

KORI. Nobody's side. I'm sick of everybody judging everybody else. It's like some big courtroom and everyone thinks they can decide what's okay and what's not.

MATT. I'm not judging anybody.

KORI. Yes, you are. You don't even realize it.

MATT. Look. I don't care who's gay and who isn't.

KORI. As long as it's not you.

MATT. I don't want to be hated for something I'm not.

KORI. Imagine what it would be like to be hated for what you are.

(REF blows whistle, signals #19, says, "Two points." Ensemble shifts.)

MATT. I'm gonna do a double workout today, double steam room, then jog home.

KORI. Maybe you ought to give them something else to talk about.

MATT. Like what?

KORI. You could hook up with somebody. Then they'd know you like girls.

MATT. I hang around you, don't I?

KORI. And I've loved you since kindergarten. But we're friends. That's all. You need to get hooked up with somebody. Connected. Nobody talked about you when you were with what's her name.

MATT. Sandy.

KORI. Yeah. That's her.

MATT. She was okay.

KORI. If you're a Neanderthal.

MATT. You don't have to rub it in.

KORI. Look, if you were dating someone, they'd have something new to focus on and they'd forget the old stuff, that's all.

MATT. Wait a minute.

KORI. Every now and then I have a decent suggestion. And there must be some girl you're hot for, if you're not hot for Luke.

MATT. Melanie Garcia.

KORI. Melanie?

MATT. Yeah, it's perfect.

KORI. I know you think she's hot. You only said it about a hundred times.

MATT. That'd take care of the rumors. She's slept with every jock in the school. "Cherry" Garcia.

(REF blows whistle, indicates MELANIE in spotlight.)

MELANIE. You think you know me, but you don't.

(REF blows whistle twice to resume. Ensemble shifts.)

KORI. Don't call her "Cherry." I like her. She's always
nice to me.

MATT. She's nice to everyone.

KORI. You think she'll go out with you? You're not exactly her type.

MATT. What do you mean by that?

KORI. Well, look at the guys she's dated, most notably
your nemesis, Willy. He's like a walking testosterone ad.
Want me to ask her if she's interested in you?

MATT. No, thanks. I can get my own dates.

KORI. Right. That's why you've had so many this year.

MATT. What's that supposed to mean?

KORI. My. Aren't we defensive. I didn't mean anything.

MATT. I've got other priorities.

KORI. Yeah. Wrestling. Wrestling and, oh yeah, I almost
forgot, wrestling.

MATT. This year's my year, Kori. I don't wanna blow it.

KORI. You mean your mom'll kill you.

MATT. That, too.

KORI. So don't ask Melanie out. We'll think of something
else. Hey, where you going?

MATT. I've gotta study pre-calc.

KORI. Eat something, will you? You look terrible. And tell
Luke to call me, okay?

MATT. I can't. Every time I see him, he runs in the oppo-
site direction.

KORI. This isn't good. I don't like this at all.

MATT. He thinks it's true. What they're saying about me. It's not true, Kori. It's not.

KORI. Okay. Okay. Who are you trying to convince?

(Buzzer. KORI exits off the mat. MATT does a series of push-ups, then spits into a can. He is dizzy, stumbles, drops. Ensemble reacts. LUKE helps MATT. MATT revives. Ensemble whispers. MATT and LUKE move away from each other.)

MATT. I'm all right. I can handle this. I know what to do.

(REF blows whistle, signals #12, says, "Caution." Ensemble continues whispering. REF repeats signal and command. Ensemble shifts. REF blows whistle, indicates MELANIE.)

MELANIE. Are you sure you're all right?

MATT. Yeah. Probably just dehydrated. You know, drying out before the wrestle-offs. Gotta make weight at 160.

MELANIE. Want some gum?

MATT. Is it sugarless?

MELANIE. Of course.

MATT. Thanks.

MELANIE. You guys are worse than the cheerleaders about your weight.

MATT. We gotta qualify.

MELANIE. What did you want to talk to me about? *(Pause.)* You said you wanted to talk to me.

MATT. I really like that ... what you're wearing.

MELANIE. My shirt?

MATT. Yeah. Your shirt. You look good.

MELANIE. Thanks. It's kind of new.

MATT. Yeah. I never saw it before.

MELANIE. That's because it's new.

MATT. You want to do something Friday night?

MELANIE. With you?

MATT. Yeah, with me.

MELANIE. Are you asking me out?

MATT. Sounds like that to me. How about it?

MELANIE. Okay, I guess.

MATT. You don't sound very enthusiastic.

MELANIE. I'm just surprised, that's all.

MATT. Because ...

MELANIE. I don't know. We don't run with the same crowd.

MATT. Look. If you don't want to go, that's okay. It was probably a bad idea anyway.

MELANIE. It's not a bad idea. I'd like to go out with you. I just never thought you'd ask me.

(REF blows whistle, indicates MATT and MELANIE. They assume the neutral position to wrestle. REF blows whistle to begin. MATT and MELANIE thumb wrestle.

REF stops thumb wrestling, blows whistle to begin again. MATT and MELANIE assume wrestling stance. MATT tickles MELANIE. REF blows whistle, signals #7, says, "Out of Bounds."

REF blows whistle. MATT and MELANIE assume the position again. They wrestle, then melt into each other and slow dance. REF, amused, gently separates them, raises their hands in the air, says, "Tie."

JOLT wrestles WILLY onto the mat.)

JOLT. You're looking mighty happy today.

WILLY. Who, me?

JOLT. Yeah, you.

WILLY. Luke was really rattled at practice yesterday.

JOLT. He lost it completely.

WILLY. He didn't have a prayer.

JOLT. It was solid, no doubt about it.

WILLY. Like taking candy from a baby.

JOLT. I wouldn't say that, but you were good, real good.

WILLY. Did you see Melanie watching me?

JOLT. Yeah. She took it in all right.

WILLY. She wants me back, I can tell.

HEATHER. You guys make me sick. Should we tell them, Nicki?

NICOLE. Yeah. Tell them.

HEATHER. I don't know. I hate to burst their bubble.

NICOLE. Yeah, but it's not fair not to tell. You have to.

(MATT and MELANIE whisper and laugh as if at a private joke.)

WILLY. What's this about?

HEATHER. Melanie, of course.

WILLY. What about Melanie?

HEATHER. I don't think she's coming to practice to see you, Willy.

NICOLE. I don't think so, either.

HEATHER. I saw her coming out of the movies Friday night with someone else.

NICOLE. This is unbelievable. It's so good.

WILLY. Who?

HEATHER. A certain wrestler named Matt.

JOLT. What? What would Melanie be doing with a loser like him.

HEATHER. I don't know, but ... she was wearing his jacket.

NICOLE. Maybe she was cold.

HEATHER. Maybe she was hot.

WILLY. For him?

JOLT. He was probably on his way to meet Luke.

WILLY. Yeah. They must have met there by accident. Did you see them go in together?

HEATHER. No, but that doesn't explain why I saw them walking together after practice yesterday.

NICOLE. It's true. I was with her.

(MATT and MELANIE cross in view of the others. MELANIE tackles MATT. He responds playfully. Ensemble shifts.)

JOLT. Wait. You think she's been coming to practice to see him?

WILLY. Yeah, right. Never happen.

JOLT. Melanie wouldn't be dating a loser like him. Besides, he's not her type.

NICOLE. Maybe they're madly, passionately in love like the poets. You know, platonic love, like in the movies.

HEATHER. You're scaring me, Nicole.

NICOLE. Well, it's possible.

HEATHER. No, it isn't.

WILLY. He's a jerk.

HEATHER. Maybe you're not the stud you thought you were, Wilbur.

NICOLE. Yeah. Some Romeo you are, Wilbur.

HEATHER. Lose your girl to Matt and Luke.

WILLY. Shut up, Heather.

JOLT. She's got it for you, man, don't worry.

WILLY. Yeah. I broke up with her, remember?

HEATHER. We'll see.

NICOLE. Yeah. We'll see.

*(Buzzer. WILLY and JOLT, NICOLE and HEATHER off
the mat. REF blows whistle, indicates MATT and
MELANIE.)*

MATT. You coming to practice again today?

MELANIE. Wouldn't miss it.

MATT. I like having you there.

MELANIE. Me and all the other wrestling groupies, huh?

MATT. I don't even see them.

MELANIE. You're too busy staring down Willy.

MATT. That's right. You coming over tonight after practice? I guarantee my mom'll ask you to stay for dinner.
She likes you.

MELANIE. Will you eat something?

MATT. Right. I can eat if I do a double workout and sit in
the steam room for an hour.

MELANIE. I can't believe I'm going out with a wrestler.
Let's break up and then get back together when wrestling season's over.

MATT. If you want to.

MELANIE. Do you want to?

MATT. Do you?

MELANIE. I asked you first.

MATT. Not a chance.

MELANIE. I worry about you, though. Pushing yourself
too far.

MATT. You sound like my mother.

MELANIE. I wouldn't want to do that.

MATT. You don't look like my mother.

MELANIE. That's good.

MATT. You don't smell like my mother, either.

MELANIE. That's good, too.

(MATT play wrestles MELANIE. She wrestles him back. MATT playfully pins her.)

MATT. You're pretty strong.

MELANIE. For a girl?

MATT. For anyone. Will you come over tonight?

MELANIE. Okay. And if you eat something, I'll work out with you after dinner.

MATT. You're amazing, you know that? Different than I thought you'd be.

MELANIE. How different?

MATT. I don't know. You just are.

MELANIE. So are you.

MATT. Good different or bad different?

MELANIE. Good different. I thought maybe you'd be like Willy.

MATT. Whoa. Stop right there.

MELANIE. You're not like Willy.

MATT. Say that again.

MELANIE. You're not like Willy. I don't think the two of us ever really did have a conversation.

MATT. Maybe you were too busy to talk.

MELANIE. What do you mean by that?

MATT. Nothing. Forget it. I don't care about what you did before.

MELANIE. What I did before?

MATT. You know, with Willy and those other guys.

MELANIE. You forgive me.

MATT. Yeah.

MELANIE. For sleeping with Willy and those other guys.

MATT. Yeah.

MELANIE. How do you know who I slept with?

MATT. You and Willy were famous. Legend.

MELANIE. You shouldn't believe what everyone says. Not all of it's true.

(Buzzer. REF blows whistle, signals #2, says, "Warning" directly to HEATHER, as she crosses onto the mat. REF indicates NICOLE and MELANIE. HEATHER paints MELANIE's toenails.)

NICOLE. I can't believe you're dating a wrestler.

MELANIE. I know. I know.

NICOLE. You're crazy.

MELANIE. Heather's dating a wrestler.

NICOLE. That's different. Heather and Jolt are practically married.

HEATHER. Don't say that too loud. My mom might hear you. I like this shade on you, Mel.

MELANIE. Plum Raisin. It's kind of dark.

NICOLE. It's sexy. You said you'd never go out with another wrestler as long as you lived. Remember?

MELANIE. I know, but that was before Matt.

NICOLE. Oooo.

HEATHER. What's he like?

MELANIE. I don't know. He's kind of shy.

HEATHER. Jolt doesn't have a shy bone in his body.

NICOLE. Yeah, Jolt's not exactly the shy type.

MELANIE. Yesterday, after wrestling practice, Matt and I walked over to his house and his mom asked me to stay for dinner. We actually sat down at the dining room table and ate together. Then me and Matt went for a long walk and talked until really late.

NICOLE. That sounds kind of boring, Mel.

MELANIE. It wasn't.

NICOLE. Oooo.

HEATHER. Do you know what Jolt did yesterday? He bought me one of those skimpy, underwear things. All lace.

NICOLE. No!

HEATHER. Yeah, can you believe it? We were up in my room and one thing led to another, you know ...

NICOLE. Oh, my God!

HEATHER. ... and my mom was right downstairs in the kitchen!

NICOLE. I can't believe it.

HEATHER. I was so afraid we'd get caught, but that made it even more fun.

NICOLE. I want a boyfriend just like that. It's so romantic. *(Pause.)* But I don't think I'm ready to be sexually active.

HEATHER. God, Nicki, you sound like you're reading from a textbook.

NICOLE. Well, I don't know how else to put it. I don't want the first time to be with just anyone. Maybe there's something wrong with me, but I'm kind of scared.

HEATHER. You would be.

MELANIE. You didn't meet the right guy yet, that's all.

NICOLE. You really think so?

HEATHER. Or else you're horribly repressed and probably frigid.

NICOLE. Shut up, Heather. My mom says wait, don't hurry. You'll know when it's the right time.

HEATHER. You listen to your mom?

MELANIE. I think you're smart, Nicole. Take your time.

HEATHER. Well, she doesn't want to become a member of the over eighteen club. You don't have much more time left, Nicki. Maybe you could be the president.

NICOLE. If you tell anybody, I'll die.

HEATHER. I won't tell anybody. But you better hurry up.

NICOLE. All the good guys are taken. Like Matt.

HEATHER. I'm kinda surprised you like him, Mel. I wouldn't think he was your type.

MELANIE. Yeah. It's kind of weird. He does this thing when I talk to him. He listens.

HEATHER. What?

NICOLE. That's so romantic. I want my boyfriend to listen to me.

HEATHER. Jolt loves me. He can't keep his hands off me. And he's jealous. I think it's so cute that he's jealous. As if I'd even look at another guy. Is Matt the jealous type?

MELANIE. Matt? He doesn't seem jealous. He's different.

NICOLE. Yeah, he's nice.

MELANIE. It's like ... he's my friend.

NICOLE. I want my boyfriend to be my friend.

HEATHER. That's not what she means, Nicki. Go ahead, Mel.

MELANIE. Never mind. It's nothing.

HEATHER. No, tell me, what is it?

MELANIE. Well, don't tell anyone, okay?

NICOLE. Scout's honor.

HEATHER. What is it?

MELANIE. You know how guys try to see how far they can get before you stop them? Matt ... well, he hasn't really done that.

(Knowing look between HEATHER and NICOLE.)

NICOLE. Maybe he doesn't feel good from losing all that weight.

HEATHER. That's stupid. Jolt says that wrestling season makes them all so horny they can hardly stand it.

MELANIE. It's like he's being careful, cautious for some reason.

HEATHER. Maybe.

NICOLE. Why don't you ask him?

HEATHER. She can't do that. That's stupid. You don't ask a guy something like that.

MELANIE. I kind of like it, in a way. One less thing to worry about.

HEATHER. There might be another reason.

MELANIE. What?

HEATHER. Maybe what they say about Matt and Luke is true.

NICOLE. Hey, that would explain it.

MELANIE. Why would he be going out with me if he's gay?

NICOLE. Yeah. That doesn't make any sense.

HEATHER. Unless he didn't want anyone to know. Then dating Melanie would be ... well, excuse me for saying so, Mel ... the perfect decoy.

NICOLE. Yeah, maybe he's just dating Mel so that people will think he's not gay.

HEATHER. That's really low. Drop him, Melanie. Don't let him use you like that.

MELANIE. That can't be true.

HEATHER. How else can you explain it?

NICOLE. Yeah. Why doesn't he act normal towards you?

MELANIE. Maybe he's just not a sex fiend.

HEATHER. Come on. That's not normal for a guy.

MELANIE. You're right about that.

(Silence as HEATHER and NICOLE exchange a look.)

HEATHER. Matt spends a lot of time with Luke, doesn't he.

MELANIE. Yeah. They've been friends since they were little.

HEATHER. That could be the reason.

MELANIE. What do you mean?

(Silence.)

NICOLE. I don't think she's seen it.

MELANIE. Seen what?

NICOLE. You tell her.

HEATHER. The Facebook page. "Stomp a Fag day."

NICOLE. They posted the whole plan, where to be and when …

HEATHER. Are you gonna tell this or am I?

NICOLE. You are. I was just...

HEATHER. They posted a photo of Luke's locker, you know, with faggot written on it. As if we needed proof. *(Pause.)*

NICOLE *(giggling)*. Thirty-six kids already liked it.

MELANIE. That's not funny.

HEATHER. Lighten up, Mel. It's just a joke.

NICOLE. Yeah. Nobody's gonna actually do anything.

HEATHER. I only told you because Matt hangs out with Luke and he's not a sex fiend.

(HEATHER and NICOLE share a laugh.)

NICOLE. Well, I think you should you just ask him.

HEATHER. Nicole. Don't think. I told you, that's stupid. You can't just come out and ask a guy a question like that.

NICOLE. Why not?

HEATHER. Get a boyfriend of your own before you wither up and die of old age.

NICOLE. I told you. All the good ones are taken.

HEATHER. Maybe you can have Matt after Melanie dumps him.

NICOLE. I still think he's cute even if he is gay.

HEATHER. You would.

(Buzzer. REF blows whistle, indicates JOLT and HEATH-ER to take the neutral position to start match. They circle, then engage, then embrace on the mat. REF blows whistle, signals #17, says, "Illegal Hold." JOLT and HEATHER pay no attention. REF repeats signal, "Illegal Hold." JOL T and HEA THER continue their embrace. REF indicates JOLT, signals #8, says, "Wrestler in Control.")

HEATHER. Jolt, take it easy. My mom'll be home any minute.

JOLT. Let's go upstairs.

HEATHER. I told you. My mom's on her way home.

JOLT. Please, I love you so much it hurts. Please.

HEATHER. Not now.

JOLT. Where you goin'? Come back here.

HEATHER. You're too dangerous.

JOLT. Come over here.

HEATHER. What time is it?

JOLT. You're killin' me. Take a knife and cut me. Go ahead. Put me out of my misery.

HEATHER. You don't act like you're suffering.

JOLT. I feel like I'm gonna explode, okay? Like I'm in a vise and you're squeezing it.

HEATHER. Me, squeeze it?

JOLT. Go ahead. I'm yours.

HEATHER. No. My mom's coming any minute and I know you.

JOLT. Who, me? I didn't do anything. Well, nothing you didn't want me to do.

HEATHER. That's all you ever want to do. Hey, I know something you'd like to know.

JOLT. Let's not talk, okay?

HEATHER. You never want to talk.

JOLT. Sure I do. Just not right now.

HEATHER. It's about a certain wrestler dating Mel.

JOLT. Not him. I hate that guy.

HEATHER. You're gonna love it.

JOLT. Whatever it is it won't make up for practice today.

HEATHER. What happened?

JOLT. He's down to 160, so it's me and Luke.

HEATHER. Oh, no.

JOLT. Oh, yes. I can't stand to touch that freak.

HEATHER. Well, do you want to hear what I heard or not?

JOLT. I'm gonna destroy him in the wrestle-offs.

HEATHER. I don't know about that. He pinned you twice last week in practice.

JOLT. Whose side are you on?

HEATHER. It's the truth. I was there.

JOLT. I'll get him rattled. I'll psych him out. I won't let him find an opening.

HEATHER. Don't worry. You'll take him.

JOLT. What if l don't?

HEATHER. Then you'll lose. It's not the end of the world.

JOLT. What are you talking about? Losing to one of those guys … it's humiliating.

HEATHER. I'll still love you, even if you lose.

JOLT. I won't lose. I can't.

HEATHER. Do you want to know what I heard, or not?

JOLT. I'll go low for the takedown and nail him before he can figure out what hit him.

HEATHER. Jolt. You are so annoying. You never listen to me.

JOLT. Okay. Tell me.

HEATHER. You have to promise you won't tell anybody or Melanie'll kill me.

JOLT. Okay.

HEATHER. Mel told me Matt hasn't even tried anything with her. Like he's just going out with her to impress everybody. They've never made out, got anywhere, done anything.

JOLT. He probably can't—unless he's with Luke.

(REF blows whistle, indicates MATT in spotlight.)

MATT. You think you know me, but you don't.

(Ensemble shifts position. REF blows whistle twice to resume.)

HEATHER. For a while I thought we were wrong about Matt, but now … well, there's no doubt in my mind.

JOLT. Why are we wasting time talking about those guys? Come here.

(They embrace. A door opens and slams. HEATHER and JOLT break apart, adjusting their clothes and hair. REF poses as MOM.)

HEATHER. Hi, Mom.

JOLT. Yeah. Hi, Mrs. Huntley. Want a hand with those groceries?

(Buzzer. REF signals #6, says, "No Control."

REF blows whistle, indicates MATT and WILLY to take positions. REF whistles to begin practice match. Ensemble cheers. REF blows whistle. The match begins. The two wrestlers circle, then engage. The remaining wrestling sequences are accompanied by loud, ugly music. Wrestling begins in real time, then becomes slow motion, then real time again. Ensemble response matches wrestling time. WILLY gains the advantage and takes MATT down. REF signals #19, says, "Two Points."

Buzzer. End of first period. REF confers with WILLY, blows whistle. MATT assumes the defensive position. WILLY crouches behind him, in the offensive position. REF blows whistle. Second round begins. The two wrestlers struggle. MATT manages to get out from under WILLY, and REF signals #15, says, "Reversal.")

WILLY. What? That was illegal! You touch me like that, I'll take your head off!

MATT. What's your problem? That was a legal move.

(REF blows whistle, signals, says, "Restart.")

WILLY. Even if you wrestle dirty, I can still whip your ass.

MATT. You're crazy. I didn't do anything to you.

(REF blows whistle, signals, repeats, "Restart. ")

WILLY. No way. I'm not wrestling him. I don't want him touching me.

(WILLY off the mat. Ensemble whispers, points at MATT. MATT turns to REF for help.)

MATT. Tell them. That wasn't illegal.

(REF blows whistle, raises MATT's hand, says, "Forfeit.")

WILLY. You keep your hands off me. I know about you. What you are.

(ENSEMBLE FUNCTIONS AS A CHORUS.)

HEATHER. Melanie told us.
JOLT. Melanie told everybody.
NICOLE. Everybody.
WILLY. Everybody knows about you now.

(MATT removes his headgear, throws it. Ensemble whispers, points.)

LUKE. Matt, wait.
MATT. Stay away from me, man. Just stay away.

(LUKE moves away from MATT. REF blows whistle, signals #11, says, "Stalemate." Buzzer. REF blows whistle, indicates KORI and LUKE.)

KORI. How'd you do on the history test?
LUKE. Ninety-three.
KORI. Not bad. Beats my pathetic eighty-nine.
LUKE. Yeah.
KORI. Wanna talk about it?
LUKE. What's the point?
KORI. I don't know. You might feel better.
LUKE. He doesn't get it, Kori. He doesn't have a clue.
KORI. He's too busy achieving his goals.
LUKE. Yeah. One match at a time.
KORI. You should talk to him.
LUKE. And say what? It's not that easy, Kori.
KORI. You got that right. *(Pause.)* Wouldn't it be great if everyone could just tell each other how they feel. I wish I...

LUKE. What?

KORI. Never mind.

LUKE. Kori?

KORI. Yeah?

LUKE. Sometimes I do think about...I don't know. Don't tell Matt.

KORI. I won't.

LUKE. I don't know if...I don't know what it means.

KORI. Me neither. *(Pause.)* Luke?

LUKE. What?

KORI. Sometimes I think about you.

(Buzzer. Ensemble shifts. REF blows whistle, indicates MATT and MELANIE. MELANIE curls herself around MATT. He withdraws.)

MELANIE. What's wrong?

MATT. Everything.

MELANIE. You want to talk about it?

MATT. No. *(Pause.)* Yes. *(Pause.)* No.

MELANIE. How was practice?

MATT. Bad.

MELANIE. You worried about the wrestle-offs?

MATT. You could say that.

MELANIE. You gonna go for the takedown?

MATT. I don't know. I'm better at defense.

MELANIE. I've watched you. I think you can take him.

MATT. I'm not so sure. I'm not sure of anything anymore.

MELANIE. I know you can beat Willy.

MATT. I don't want to talk about it.

MELANIE. Okay, let's not talk about wrestling. I just want to be here with you. *(Pause.)* Matt?

MATT. What?

MELANIE. Come sit with me. *(He sits. They wait. She caresses him. MATT grabs her.)* Hey, what's your hurry? *(He takes her down on the mat.)* Matt, you're hurting me.

MATT. Am I?

MELANIE. What's the matter?

MATT. Nothing.

MELANIE. Why are you acting like this?

MATT. Isn't this what you wanted?

MELANIE. Matt, stop it. *(He does not stop. He pins her.)* Stop it, Matt! Stop it!

MATT. Isn't this what you wanted?

MELANIE. Matt, no! Please! Not like this.

MATT. You told Willy I couldn't, didn't you? *(He presses himself against her until he makes his point.)* Now do you think I can? Do you? Do you?

MELANIE. Yes. Yes. Please. Let me go. *(MATT releases her. She is crying.)* What's the matter with you?

MATT. What's the matter with you?

MELANIE. I haven't even talked to Willy. And even if I did that doesn't give you the right to...to...

MATT. I thought that's what you wanted, what you did with those other guys.

MELANIE. What I did? How would you know what I did? *(Ensemble whispers in the background.)* Those guys... everyone who talks about me, they don't know me. They don't know how I feel. I never slept with anyone, Matt. No one. Not even Willy. *(She laughs through her tears.)* It's funny, isn't it? I never even wanted to be with anyone like that...except you.

MATT. Right. You expect me to believe that?

MELANIE. You can believe what you want.

MATT. Tell me what to believe.

MELANIE. I don't care anymore.

(Ensemble is silent.)

MATT. Melanie...

MELANIE. Don't touch me.

MATT. Why didn't you say something? Why did you let everybody believe you were a... *(He hesitates.)*

MELANIE. Say it. Go ahead. Say it. Slut. It's an ugly word.

MATT. How could you take all the lies about you?

MELANIE. How could I take it? I liked it. I wanted them to talk about me, all right? Nobody talked about me before. No one even knew I existed. Now guys brag about me to their friends. A lot of guys want to go out with me now. Would you have asked me out if my nickname wasn't "Cherry" Garcia? Would you? Would you? *(Silence.)* I thought so.

MATT. Melanie...I'm sorry.

MELANIE. Forget it. Why should you be any different.

MATT. Melanie, wait.

MELANIE. Finally, I meet someone who makes me feel good, like I'm special. But you know what, I made you up, you're not real. You're just like all the rest of them.

(REF blows whistle, signals #15, says, "Reversal." MELANIE joins ensemble. KORI crosses onto mat.)

KORI. Guess you blew that big time.

MATT. Don't rub it in.

KORI. She'll probably never speak to you again.

MATT. Probably.

KORI. What are you gonna do?

MATT. Beat Willy in the wrestle-offs.

KORI. I mean about Melanie.

MATT. Beat Willy in the wrestle-offs.

(Buzzer. Lights dim to dappled night. Ensemble seems to disappear in darkness. LUKE enters the space. He becomes aware he is not alone. The first blow knocks him to the ground.)

LUKE. What... *(He shields his face.)* No, don't.

(He is overpowered and pummeled in the face and body. We do not see the attackers. We experience the assault through LUKE's face and body movement. REF blows whistle, signals #21, says, "Flagrant Misconduct." LUKE crawls off the mat and exits. Restore lights. Ensemble re-emerges. REF blows whistle, indicates MATT and KORI.)

KORI. How was the weigh-in?

MATT. No problem. A piece of cake.

KORI. I see Melanie.

MATT. Where?

KORI. Don't strain yourself. She's over there.

MATT. You seen Luke?

KORI. No. Not today. I don't think he came to school.

MATT. I can't believe it. The day of the wrestle-offs.

KORI. He called me last night. He sounded pretty bad.

MATT. What did he say?

KORI. I can't tell you. Luke made me promise not to say anything.

MATT. Then why did you bring it up?

KORI. Because I'm worried. I don't like it that he didn't come to school. And where is he now?

MATT. He won't miss the wrestle-offs.

KORI. I called his house. He's not there and his mom doesn't know where he is. She's worried, too.

MATT. What time is it?

KORI. Ten after three.

MATT. It's just warm-up. The match won't start until four. He'll be here.

KORI. Matt, have you ever known Luke to miss a warm-up? I'm really worried.

MATT. Did you check the locker room?

KORI. Now, how am I going to do that?

MATT. Wait here. I'll go.

(REF indicates MATT, JOLT and WILLY.)

WILLY. Well, look who's here.

JOLT. Yeah, Mr. Can't Do Wrong.

WILLY. Who you looking for?

JOLT. Yeah, you looking for your buddy Luke?

MATT. Kiss my ass.

WILLY. I bet he is looking for Luke.

MATT. I'm not looking for anyone.

JOLT. Let me see. Luke.

WILLY. Yeah, Luke. You remember, the 171 pounder you used to wrestle.

MATT. What do you mean, used to wrestle?

WILLY. I heard he quit the team.

JOLT. Probably scared of the wrestle-offs.

WILLY. Coach said he won't be wrestling today. Guess that's a forfeit.

JOLT. Too bad. I was looking forward to a public humiliation.

WILLY. Or two.

MATT. You'd like that, wouldn't you?

JOLT. I would.

WILLY. Sounds good to me.

MATT. Where is he?

JOLT. Thought you weren't looking for him.

WILLY. And I don't see him anywhere, do you?

MATT. Where is he?

JOLT. If I knew, do you think I'd tell you?

MATT *(controls his rage)*. Thanks. You reminded me of something I almost forgot.

WILLY. Glad to oblige.

JOLT. Yeah. Always happy to be helpful.

(REF blows whistle, signals #2, says, "Time Out." Dappled light. REF leads LUKE onto the mat, wearing warm-up jacket. MATT puts on his warm-up jacket.)

MATT. God, it's cold. How long you been here?

LUKE. Since last night.

MATT. You spent the night in Gebhardt's garage? You're lucky you didn't freeze to death.

LUKE. I worked out. That helped. Old man Gebhardt nearly caught me.

MATT. Was it that stupid dog barking?

LUKE. Yeah. Gebhardt came out here with his flashlight to check. Good thing he's blind as a bat or he'd have found me for sure.

MATT. You could have come to my house. *(Silence.)* I heard you quit the team.

LUKE. Yeah. I told Coach I couldn't make the wrestle-offs.

MATT. You told him you couldn't make it? This isn't a tea party. Are you crazy?

LUKE. That's it. You've found me out. I'm crazy. So I quit.

MATT. That's not what I mean. Why'd you do it?

LUKE. I just did, that's all.

MATT. Tell me what the hell's going on. Why did you quit the team?

LUKE. Go to the wrestle-offs. You're gonna be late.

MATT. I don't have time for games, Luke.

LUKE. Then go.

MATT. You can rot here for all I care. *(MATT begins to leave, then stops.)* Wait a minute. Not this time. You're pretty slick, Luke, but I'm not going without you. *(He goes to LUKE. LUKE pulls off his hood. Light falls on LUKE's bloodied face.)* Aw, God, Luke. Who did this to you?

LUKE. There were two of them.

MATT. Two of them?

LUKE. They were wearing masks. I don't know for sure. It might have been them.

MATT. Why didn't you tell me?

LUKE. I didn't want to make things worse than they already are.

MATT. You should have told me.

LUKE. So you could do what?

MATT. Beat them both to a bloody pulp. One at a time.

LUKE. That's what I thought.

MATT. What do you expect me to do?

LUKE. Go to the wrestle-offs and pin Willy.

MATT. And leave you here? No way.

LUKE. I'll be okay.

MATT. I'm not leaving you here.

LUKE. You'd be better off if you did.

MATT. What's that supposed to mean?

LUKE. Do you think all this would have happened if we weren't friends?

MATT. This isn't your fault. It could have happened to anybody.

LUKE. But it happened to me.

MATT. So?

LUKE. Don't you know why? They got me pegged. Pinned. Figured out. I'm a freak. And everybody knows it.

MATT. You're not a freak. They don't even know you.

LUKE. Maybe they do. Maybe they know something I don't.

MATT. They don't know anything.

LUKE. What if it's true about me? Have you ever thought about that?

MATT. No, I haven't.

LUKE. Well, maybe you should.

MATT *(prowls)*. Listen to me. I know you. The rest of it doesn't matter. Not to me. *(Silence.)* It's freezing in here.

LUKE. Sorry I deserted you on the pre-calc test.

MATT. That's okay. I passed anyway.

LUKE. I thought if I stayed away it would be better.

MATT. You gonna hide out here for the rest of your life?

LUKE. No.

MATT. Good. Because I'm sick of freezing my butt off talking to you. Let's get you cleaned up. We don't have much time.

LUKE. I'm scared.

MATT. I know. It got to me, too. But Jolt and Willy reminded me who the good guys are. Come on. I'm not taking no for an answer. Get up.

LUKE. You're worse than your mom. You're a maniac.

MATT. That's right. Let's go.

LUKE. I'm not sure I can win.

MATT. I'm not either. But if you don't try then they win for sure. *(Holds out his hand to LUKE, helps him to his feet.)* If Jolt kills you, I'll donate your body to science.

(Buzzer. REF signals #19, says, "Two Points." Restore lights. MATT helps LUKE off the mat. JOLT and LUKE put on headgear, warm up for match.)

ENSEMBLE *(cheer).*
    Tick, tick, tick, tick, tick, tick, tick.
    Hold up, wait a minute, put a little boom in it,
    Boom, dynamite,
    Boom, boom, dynamite
    Boom, dynamite,
    Boom, boom.
    When you mess with dynamite,
    It goes like this...
    Tick, tick, tick, tick, tick, tick, tick, tick...BOOM!

(REF blows whistle, indicates JOLT and LUKE to take positions for the match. REF blows whistle. Wrestlers

shake hands. REF checks LUKE's face, blows whistle to start match. Music and real time, slow motion, real time as suggested before. JOLT shoots low and takes LUKE down. JOLT struggles to pin LUKE but LUKE twists out of JOLT's grip and escapes. Buzzer. End of first period. REF signals #19, says, "Two Points."

REF blows whistle, indicates LUKE, who takes the defensive position. JOLT kneels behind him. REF blows whistle to begin second period. JOLT tries to flip LUKE onto his back. They struggle. LUKE gains control. JOLT works himself out of bounds. REF blows whistle, signals #7, says, "Out of Bounds."

REF blows whistle, JOLT takes the defensive position, LUKE on top. JOLT rolls LUKE, gains control. The two wrestlers strain against each other. REF lies down on the mat to watch for the pin.)

ENSEMBLE. Ten ... nine ... eight ... seven ... six ...

(REF shouts: "One, two," slaps the mat. Buzzer. LUKE is defeated. JOLT jumps to his feet. Ensemble cheers. LUKE lies on the mat, then gets to his feet. REF blows whistle, indicates wrestlers shake hands. LUKE and JOLT touch hands. REF holds JOLT's hand in the air, indicating a win. Ensemble cheers. LUKE removes headgear and is comforted by KORI.)

ENSEMBLE *(cheer)*.
Don't mess, don't mess,
Don't mess with the best,

'Cause the best don't mess.
Don't fool, don't fool,
Don't fool with the cool,
'Cause the cool don't fool.
To the east, to the west,
Willy is the best, best, best!

(REF blows whistle, indicates MATT and WILLY. They take the starting position, staring each other down.)

WILLY. You ready for this?
MATT. Ready? No, I'd say eager describes it better.

(REF signals wrestlers shake hands. REF blows whistle to start match. Wrestlers lock arms, competing for the takedown. Each endeavors to gain control but they are evenly matched. WILLY takes MATT down. REF signals #19, says, "Two Points." MATT tries to escape but WILLY flips him on his back, forcing his shoulders onto the mat. WILLY gets MATT in a painful scissor hold. The crowd cheers, anticipating a pin. MATT gains control, flips WILLY onto his back. REF signals one point for the escape. Ensemble cheers, as MATT pushes WILLY closer and closer to the mat. The ref counts: "One, two," and slaps the mat, indicating a pin. Buzzer.)

ENSEMBLE *(cheer)*.
    Hey, Matt, what's your cry?
    V-I-C-T-O-R-Y! Go-o-o, Matt!

(WILLY gets up, barely containing his fury. REF signals wrestlers to shake hands. MATT holds out his hand and

WILLY grazes it. REF blows whistle, raises MATT's arm to indicate victory. Ensemble cheers.)

JOLT. This isn't over yet. One down. One to go.

MATT. We could settle this right now.

WILLY. Sounds like a good idea to me.

LUKE. Let's go, Matt.

MATT. Move out of the way. You're in no shape to get in the middle of this.

JOLT. Haven't you had enough?

LUKE. Matt, this is what he wants.

MATT. No, it's what I want.

LUKE. If you do this you'll be disqualified. Willy'll step into your slot.

MATT. I don't care.

LUKE. I do.

MATT. Move out of the way, Luke.

JOLT. Yeah, move out of the way, Luke.

LUKE. Remember what you said to me? We gotta stick together or they'll win. I'm not moving. You'll have to go through me to get to him.

JOLT. I'd like to see that.

LUKE. You won here today. *(Pause.)* And so did I.

KORI. Luke's right. They're not worth the hassle.

LUKE. Let's go.

JOLT. Guess you two have better things to do than fight, huh?

MATT *(grabs JOLT in a choke hold)*. Look at him. Look at him! Do you know the guts it took for him to show up here? If you ever lay a hand on my friend again, I'll stick you to the mat so hard you'll never get up.

(REF blows whistle, thinks, signals #8, says, "Wrestler in Control." MATT releases JOLT.)

JOLT. We didn't do it, man. I don't know who nailed your friend, but it wasn't us.

(Ensemble shifts. REF indicates MELANIE and KORI.)

MELANIE. Guess you're gonna celebrate tonight, huh?

KORI. Yeah. I guess so. *(Pause.)* You wanna join us?

MELANIE. No, thanks.

KORI. I'm sorry about you and Matt.

MELANIE. It's not your fault.

KORI. I'm sorry anyway. Did he hurt you?

MELANIE. He told you what happened?

KORI. He's really upset about it. Are you okay?

MELANIE. Yeah. No. I thought he really cared about me. That's a joke, huh? Someone like Matt caring for someone like me?

KORI. It's not a joke.

MELANIE. Yes, it is. It's the joke of the century. And I set it up. I let them talk about me that way. Melanie's hot. She'll go for it. He thought that's what I wanted. I deserved what I got.

KORI. No, you didn't. You didn't deserve to be the target of Matt's insane determination. Nobody deserves that.

MELANIE. I only wanted him to... *(KORI reaches for her, she recoils.)* You want to hear the real irony of it? I would have given him anything if he'd asked me.

KORI. Melanie?

MELANIE. Yeah?

KORI. I thought you two were good for each other. I really did.

MELANIE. Guess we were both wrong about that.

KORI. Maybe you should talk to him?

MELANIE. I wish I could just disappear.

(Silence.)

KORI. Hey, I'm going to a poetry reading tomorrow at The Barn.

MELANIE. Oh, yeah. I heard you go there a lot.

KORI. There'll be some cool people there. Want to come along?

MELANIE. I better not. I've gotta work. You know.

KORI. Yeah, I know. Maybe some other time.

MELANIE. Yeah. Sure.

(REF blows whistle, indicates KORI and MELANIE in spotlight.)

KORI & MELANIE. You think you know me, but you don't.

(Ensemble shifts. REF whistles twice to resume, indicates MATT and MELANIE.)

MATT. I did it, Melanie. I won.

MELANIE. Congratulations.

MATT. Melanie, wait.

MELANIE. Don't. My friends are waiting.

MATT. They're not your friends. *(Pause.)* I'll call you, okay?

MELANIE. I probably won't be home.

MATT. I want to talk to you, Melanie. I want to explain.

WILLY. Come on, Mel. We're getting old waiting for you.

MELANIE. I'm coming.

MATT. You're going with him?

MELANIE. Yeah.

MATT. I can't believe it. You don't even like him.

MELANIE. So what?

MATT. Melanie, give me a chance.

MELANIE. Why should I?

MATT. Because he doesn't care about you. You're just a trophy to him.

MELANIE. And you? What do you care about?

MATT. I don't know.

MELANIE. At least with Willy I know what to expect.

MATT. That's not what I meant. Melanie. I care about you. *(He reaches for her. She recoils.)* Please. Don't write me off. I know I went about this all wrong. I want to start over. I want to make it right.

HEATHER. Come on, Mel, we're waiting.

MELANIE. Heather thinks I should press charges.

MATT. What? Press charges for what? Nothing happened.

MELANIE. Nothing happened? Maybe not for you.

MATT. That's not what I meant. I shouldn't have been so rough, but I was angry. I made a mistake. I'm sorry.

MELANIE. I wish I could believe that.

MATT. Believe it. Don't press charges. Don't do that to me. Please, Melanie.

WILLY. We're leaving without you, Mel.

MATT. What are you going to do?

MELANIE. I don't know.

MATT. Don't go with him, Melanie. Let's talk this over. Please.

(MATT extends his hand. MELANIE hesitates, then takes it, drops it, joins WILLY. MATT remains alone on the mat. REF blows whistle, signals #15, says, "Reversal." REF indicates HEATHER and JOLT.)

HEATHER. Hey, my parents aren't home tonight. We could have a little celebration at my house.

JOLT. I can't. I promised the guys I'd party with them tonight. You know, wrestling buddies.

HEATHER. Oh, well, that's okay, I guess. I'll ask Nicki to sleep over. See ya tomorrow?

JOLT. Yeah, sure, baby.

(REF indicates NICOLE.)

NICOLE. Psst! Heather!

HEATHER. What?

NICOLE. Oh, God, I don't know how to tell you this. You'll die.

HEATHER. Don't be so melodramatic, Nicki. Just tell me.

NICOLE. I can't.

HEATHER. If you don't tell me, I'll strangle you right here in front of everybody.

NICOLE. You're going out with Jolt tonight, aren't you?

HEATHER. As a matter of fact, no. Why?

NICOLE. Oh, God.

HEATHER. Nicki, give it up.

NICOLE. Liz and Anne Marie are meeting Jolt at the diner.

HEATHER. What?

NICOLE. Oh, God...I can't tell you.

HEATHER. Tell me!

NICOLE. I heard that Liz can't wait anymore to tell him that she's... *(NICOLE whispers to HEATHER.)*

HEATHER. Shut up.

NICOLE. What?

HEATHER. I said shut up. You must have heard wrong.

NICOLE. But she said...

HEATHER. Jolt loves me. He hasn't slept with Liz or anyone else.

(REF blows whistle, indicates JOLT in spotlight.)

JOLT. You think you know me, but you don't.

(REF whistles twice to resume. Ensemble shifts.)

NICOLE. Okay. Okay. But I know what I heard.

HEATHER. No, you don't.

NICOLE. Yes, I do.

HEATHER. No, you don't.

NICOLE. Well, I guess I could have heard wrong.

HEATHER. That's right.

(Buzzer. REF signals #1, says, "End of Match." Ensemble is grouped at center of mat.)

REFEREE. Because sportsmanship always takes priority over winning, and because losing is a lesson which must be learned early in life...

(ENSEMBLE FUNCTIONS AS A CHORUS.)

ALL *(except REFEREE)*. I will remember always that fair play, moral obligation and ethics are a part of winning and losing, that graciousness and humility should always characterize a winner and that pride and honor do not desert a good loser.

(Ensemble speaks directly to the audience.)

HEATHER. You think you know the way it is.
JOLT. You think you know the score.
NICOLE. You think you're so smart.
KORI. You think you've got me figured out.
WILLY. You think you've got me pegged. Pinned.
MELANIE. You think you know me, but you don't.
LUKE. How can you know me?
ENSEMBLE *(except REFEREE)*. I'm not even sure I know myself.

(Ensemble stands facing the audience as lights fade slowly to ...)

BLACKOUT—END PLAY

Post Performance Forum
Designed by Laurie Brooks

If the theatre decides to employ the forum, there is no curtain call directly following the performance. Instead, following the final blackout, the audience is greeted by the facilitator, who introduces himself and invites them to participate in a brief post-performance experience. The forum can be as long as an hour or as short as twenty minutes. The facilitator then takes audience members through five steps that encourage them to travel deeper into the issues, emotions, and characters in the play. The play may be performed with or without the forum. The audience experience is enhanced by the forum, but the play stands on its own.

Part I. AGREE and DISAGREE STATEMENTS:

As the Facilitator reads each statement, audience members are asked to stand in support if they agree or remain seated in protest if they disagree. This all-group opening exercise provides safe expression of audience opinions and strong visual images regarding character actions in the play.

1. Melanie should get back together with Matt.

2. Jolt is lying when he says that he and Willy aren't the ones who beat up Luke.

3. Rumors can be hurtful but they usually don't cause any lasting damage.

4. Kori's suggestion that Matt hook up with someone to help dispel the rumors was ill-advised.

5. Even though he stands by Luke, Matt is still homophobic.

6. Most people believe rumors without making the effort to discover the truth.

7. The pressure to succeed that Matt feels in the play is mostly self-generated.

8. Heather got what she deserves at the end of the play.

Part II. RANKING

Facilitator invites the characters from the play to join the proceedings.

After the characters are introduced, audience members rank their behavior in the play from most objectionable to least objectionable. Facilitator places the characters in a line from most objectionable behavior to least objectionable according to audience ranking, providing a visual reference.

Facilitator then calls on individual audience members to adjust the rankings according to their personal opinions. Facilitator will re-adjust the characters in the lineup, asking volunteers to share their reasons for ranking the characters as indicated. This affords the opportunity for awareness of differing opinions.

Part III. GROUP RESPONSE

Characters respond to audience ranking. Taking turns, the group speaks about their actions and motivations in the play. These brief speeches may be rehearsed, improvised or a combination of both. They may take the form of an apology, thoughts about what audience members have said, or defending their actions in the play. It is important that this segment not become didactic, but that the characters speak from their personal points of view. Now the audience has new information about the characters. One character does not speak but is withheld for closure.

Part IV. REFLECTION

Audience members are asked to share sentences or phrases of comfort, advice, affirmation or counsel to the characters in the play. In this portion of the forum, the facilitator stands back, allowing participants to negotiate this segment themselves. Audience members stand, one at a time, offer brief thoughts, then sit, taking turns until all who choose to participate have had an opportunity to speak. The characters are silent throughout, listening.

Part V. CLOSURE

The character who did not speak earlier now brings the workshop to a close with thoughts about his or her actions and motivations in the play, or perhaps some commentary about what the audience members have said. It is important to end this closing step on a positive note.

The facilitator thanks audience members and the characters for their participation, encouraging applause for themselves and the actors. Curtain call.

END OF FORUM

Facilitator's Guide

After the actors exit, the facilitator greets the audience and invites them to participate in the forum. It is crucial that the facilitator not make any judgments, positive or negative, regarding audience responses in the forum. He/She remains neutral throughout.

Sample Dialogue:

FACILITATOR. Good afternoon, and welcome to *The Wrestling Season*. I'd like to invite you now to participate in a unique theatre forum where we'll ask you to share some of your opinions and thoughts about the issues raised in the play.

Part I. AGREE AND DISAGREE STATEMENTS

This step should move quickly. No discussion. If someone wants to speak, ask him/her to hold the question/comment for later.

Sample Dialogue:

FACILITATOR. I'm going to read a series of statements about some of the actions in the play and I want you to stand in support if you agree or stay seated in protest if you disagree.

Facilitator thanks the audience for their participation after each statement, asking them to sit down before beginning the next. Facilitator may offer neutral comments on audience response.

Sample Dialogue:

FACILITATOR. That looks fairly unanimous to me.
                        or:
   I think that's about half and half.

NOTE: In the premiere production, the referee took on the role of facilitator, so in this description the pronoun "he" will be used for simplicity. However, facilitating this forum is equally effective done by a woman.

Part II. RANKING

The facilitator brings the actors back into the space, never referring to them as actors but, rather, calling them "the characters" or "the group." He asks them to introduce themselves and, in character, the actors state their names. Facilitator then explains that he will determine the ranking of the characters by the volume of a "yes" response as each character's name is called. Again, no discussion at this point. This is still information gathering.

Sample Dialogue:

FACILITATOR. When I point to someone in the group you'll help me determine how to rank their behavior from most objectionable to least objectionable by the volume of your yeses. Did you object to Nicole's behavior?

After all the characters have been named, the facilitator brings onstage four or five characters, placing them in order based on the strongest responses on objectionable behavior. He then reverses the process, asking the audience to rank the four or five characters based on behavior that meets with their approval.

FACILITATOR. Did you approve of Kori's behavior?

The facilitator states he has attempted to best represent the majority viewpoint regarding the characters' behavior. He now calls upon several audience members with differing opinions to re-rank the group, stating their reasons.

FACILITATOR. This is how I think you, the audience, has ranked the group. But some of you may feel differently about the ranking. Who would like to stand and give us your re-ranking and reasons why?

Remaining in character, the group of actors rearrange themselves to represent the new rankings.

Toward the end of the ranking, when Kori has been placed in the number one or two slot for least objectionable behavior, she makes a confession.

KORI. Hold up. I've got something to say. I belong down there. *(She indicates the other end of the ranking.)* I don't think I'd be ranked here if you guys knew.

FACILITATOR. Okay. Go ahead, Kori.

KORI. I saw that stuff on Facebook, and I didn't do anything about it. That makes me responsible, too, doesn't it?

LUKE *(quietly shocked)*. You knew?

MELANIE. It's not your fault, Kori. I knew and I didn't tell anyone. I didn't take it seriously. I thought it was a joke.

KORI. But it's like … seeing somebody get hit by a car and just walking away from it.

(SILENCE. FACILITATOR waits for the audience to re-spond. If no one does, use the following.)

FACILITATOR *(to audience)*. What do you think? Do you think this changes the ranking?

(If, after the above, someone asks KORI why she didn't tell someone, use the following.

KORI takes a moment to find her courage.)

KORI. I was scared, okay? They already think I'm gay. I was afraid they'd come after me. I mean, that's what happens, isn't it, when you've got a giant target on your back? I walk home alone from school every day. Guess I was too busy protecting myself to think about anyone else.

Part III. GROUP RESPONSE

Sample Dialogue:

FACILITATOR. Now I'm going to give the group a chance to respond to your ranking them in this order.

One at a time, the characters speak. (As noted above, the characters speak about their actions and motivations in the play. These brief speeches may be rehearsed, improvised or a combination of both. They may take the form of an apology, thoughts about what audience members have said or defending their actions in the play.)

Sample Dialogue:

NICOLE. I just want to say that regardless of anyone's behavior, I don't think that Heather deserved what she got. No one deserves that. (Audience response.) Do any of you deserve that?

WILLY. I want to take responsibility for my actions and I think everyone up here should do the same.

MELANIE. I know people make mistakes and I know that it was a mistake that allowed the rumors about me, but people don't have to believe them.

JOLT. I see now what you guys are talking about. When you say stuff it means something to someone else. It's a bigger deal to them than it is to you. But I think it's really sad that some of you say you can't forgive. I mean, I'm really sorry about what I did to Heather and I just hope she can forgive me.

Part IV. REFLECTION

After stating the guidelines, the facilitator will step into the background during this portion of the workshop. He asks audience members not to raise their hands but to negotiate their responses by simply standing and taking turns. The facilitator allows many comments, allowing the reflection to build over the course of ten minutes or more. Sensing a wrap-up moment, the facilitator waits for someone to make an especially cogent or pointed comment and stops the action.

The facilitator lays out these guidelines for the participants.

1. No name-calling. If someone breaks this rule, don't let it go by. Stop the action and ask the participants what they think of that behavior. They will self-patrol the action. The facilitator models appropriate language.

2. No cursing. Facilitator responds as above.

3. Use "I" messages. "You" is accusatory and puts everyone on the defensive. This rule offers a message to young people about effective communication.

Sample Dialogue:

FACILITATOR. Just like at school, there'll be no cursing or name-calling. Can we agree on that? (Audience response.) I'm not sure about that response. Can we agree to no cursing and no name-calling? (Audience response— more enthusiastic.) Thank you. It's important to start with the word "I," like I think or I feel...and follow that with your phrase or sentence to someone in the group.

After comments are complete, the facilitator thanks the audience and states he would like to conclude the forum. At this time, the actor who has not spoken now says s/he would like to speak.

Part V. CLOSURE

The final character speaks. Which character closes the workshop may be determined before the proceedings.

Sample Dialogue:

KORI. You know what, it doesn't matter if Jolt and Willy did or didn't do it. They still caused it. They created an atmosphere of hate that made it possible for someone to think it was okay to go after Luke. Look at that locker! That word hit him harder than the fists, whoever they belonged to. Matt, I had no right to suggest that you ask Melanie out just to stop the rumors. If I had known that something like this would happen, I never would have said such a dumb thing. But hindsight is 20/20, isn't it?

The Facilitator ends the forum.

FACILITATOR. Thank you, audience, for your great participation today. I want to take a moment now to introduce you to (names the intervention specialist or counselor in attendance) who has more information for you and your teachers on the way out. And now, give yourselves and the cast of *The Wrestling Season* a big hand.

Comments from Jeff Church, Producing Artistic Director, The Coterie Theatre, Kansas City, Missouri, about his experience directing _The Wrestling Season._

• An actual wrestling coach is vital. If you should be lucky enough to find someone who can be at every rehearsal and has theatre experience, you'll be even better off. The best scenario, we found, was to give the company a vocabulary of wrestling movements they could draw upon throughout the staging of the play. We kept much of the action low to the mat and played against traditional or realistic "high school hallway" staging.

• Using wrestling singlets for all, no matter what vocal reaction the audience has in the beginning, is worth it overall.

• Peppered throughout the play is: "You think you know me, but you don't." These worked best when the characters spoke directly to the other characters instead of direct address—yet, the referee's spoken explanation of his signals worked best given to the audience.

• Laurie's play being an anti-model, the logical extension of this played out in rehearsal when the characters with the most deplorable behavior became fully justified in their own minds—and filling their actions with dimension became important. (The villains weren't villains, and the victims weren't played as victims.)

• In the post performance forum, you'll want a series of test audiences throughout rehearsals for the referee and the group. Waiting for previews to begin the forum would have been a mistake. We found the forum was very much an ongoing process, and we were adjusting and refining it throughout the run.

• The audience may finally realize that the ranking section of the forum ironically puts them in the position of judging the characters—and we found people having strong feelings about this to be okay. The referee is simply there to allow them to air their feelings, not to teach or justify the forum.